The
Baby's Catalogue

Janet and Allan Ahlberg

Viking

VIKING

Published by the Penguin Group
Penguin Books Ltd, 27 Wrights Lane, London W8 5TZ, England
Penguin Books USA Inc., 375 Hudson Street, New York, New York 10014, USA
Penguin Books Australia Ltd, Ringwood, Victoria, Australia
Penguin Books Canada Ltd, 10 Alcorn Avenue, Toronto, Ontario, Canada M4V 3B2
Penguin Books (NZ) Ltd, 182–190 Wairau Road, Auckland 10, New Zealand

Penguin Books Ltd, Registered Offices: Harmondsworth, Middlesex, England

First published in 1982
11 13 15 17 19 20 18 16 14 12

ISBN 0-670-80895-4

Printed in Great Britain by
William Clowes Ltd, Beccles and London

Contents

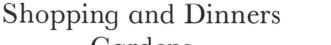
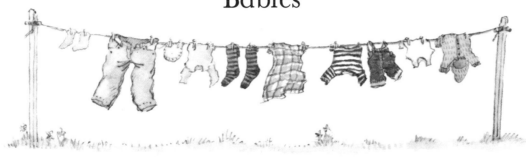

For Jessica

 # Babies

Dads

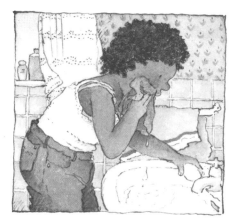

Mums

Mornings

High Chairs

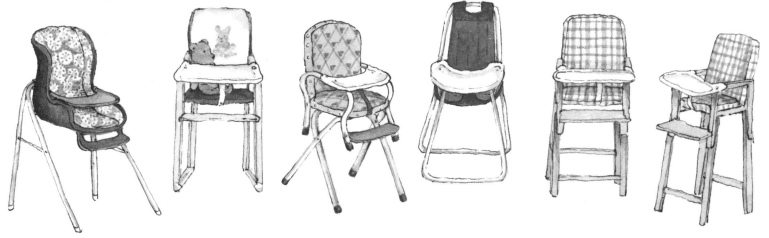

Breakfasts

Toys

Teddy	Bricks	Rattle	Top
Tricycle	Doll	Car	Ducks
Frog	Trolley	Elephant	Ball

Brothers and Sisters

Prams

Swings

Nappies

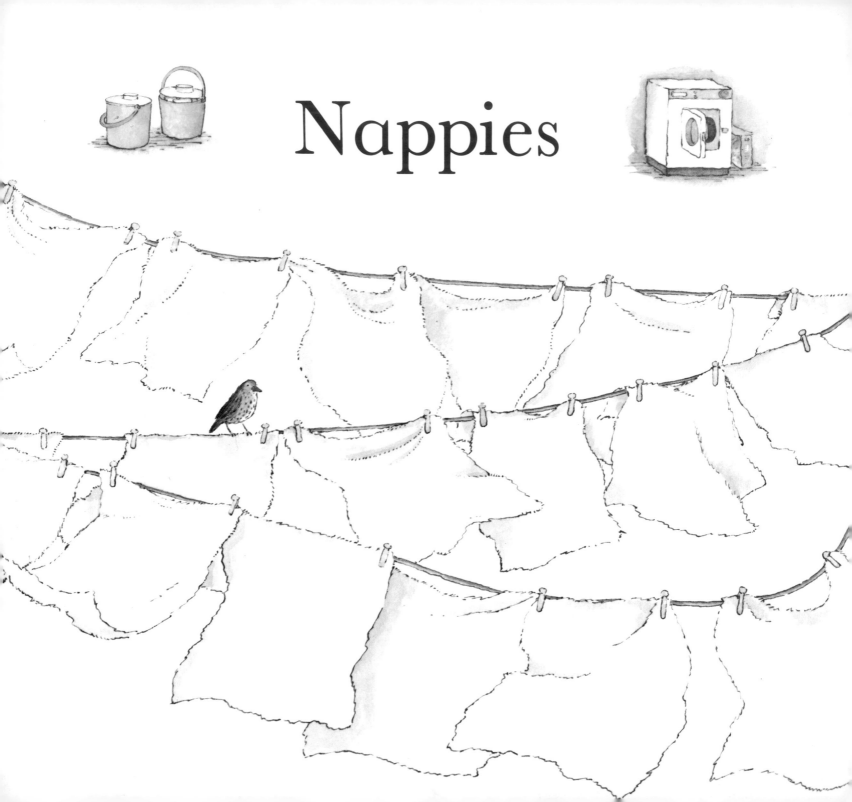

Bouncing

Piggyback

Catching

Games

Climbing

Peepo!

Boo!

 # Shopping

Fruit

Tins

Baby Things

Sausages

Boxes

 # Dinners

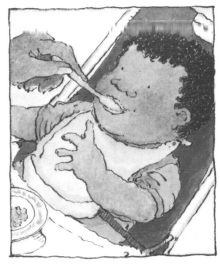

Gardens

Flowers	Bird	Lettuce	Butterfly
Dustbin	Mower	Spider	Watering Can
Spade	Washing	Pots	Grass

Paddling Pool

Sandpit

Accidents

Mirrors

Pets

Dog	Hamster	Frog	Rabbit
Budgie	Goldfish	Cat	Mouse
Kittens	Caterpillar	Dog	Guinea Pig

Ants

Teas

Cups

Pots

Bread

Salad

Cakes

Books

Baths

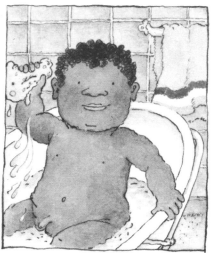

 # Bedtimes

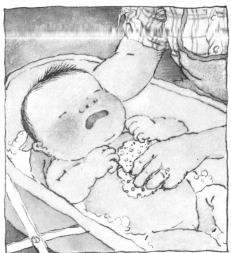

Mums and Dads

Babies

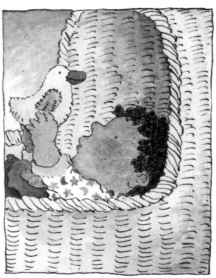

The End